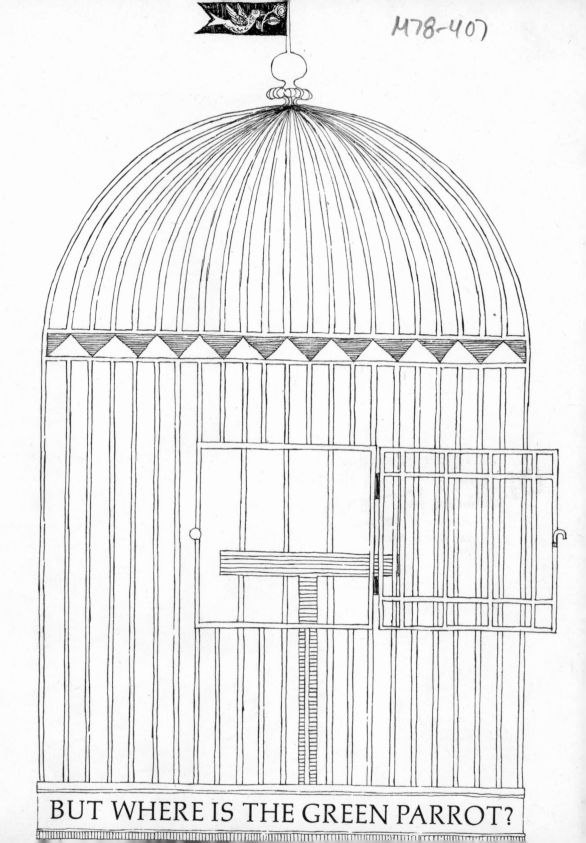

BUT WHERE IS THE GREEN PARROT?

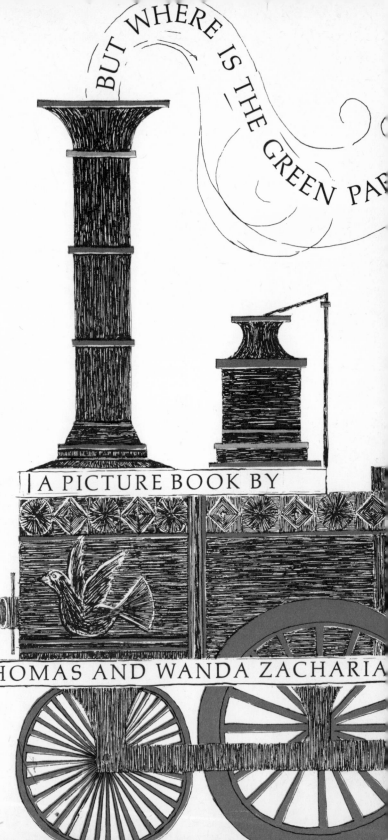

BUT WHERE IS THE GREEN PARROT?

A PICTURE BOOK BY

THOMAS AND WANDA ZACHARIAS

A Seymour Lawrence Book
Delacorte Press
New York

THE TRAIN

has a black engine
with red wheels,
an engine-driver
with a blue coat and cap,

a yellow coach with many windows—

BUT WHERE IS THE GREEN PARROT?

THE HOUSE
has a red roof
with a chimney,
a blue door
with a latch,
a yellow balcony
with flowerpots—
BUT WHERE IS THE GREEN PARROT?

THE TOY CHEST
has a red ball
to throw,
bright wooden blocks
to build with,
a yellow teddy bear
to love —
BUT WHERE IS THE GREEN PARROT?

THE TABLE
has a pink tablecloth
with flowers,
chocolate cake
on a yellow plate,
milk in a blue
mug—

BUT WHERE IS THE GREEN PARROT?

THE GARDEN
has a big tree
heavy with red apples,
a boat
sailing in a birdbath,
a watering can
for the yellow flowers—
BUT WHERE IS THE GREEN PARROT?

THE HORSE
has a red mane
with tight curls,
a blue bridle
with yellow tassels,
a rider in the saddle
with high boots—
BUT WHERE IS THE GREEN PARROT?

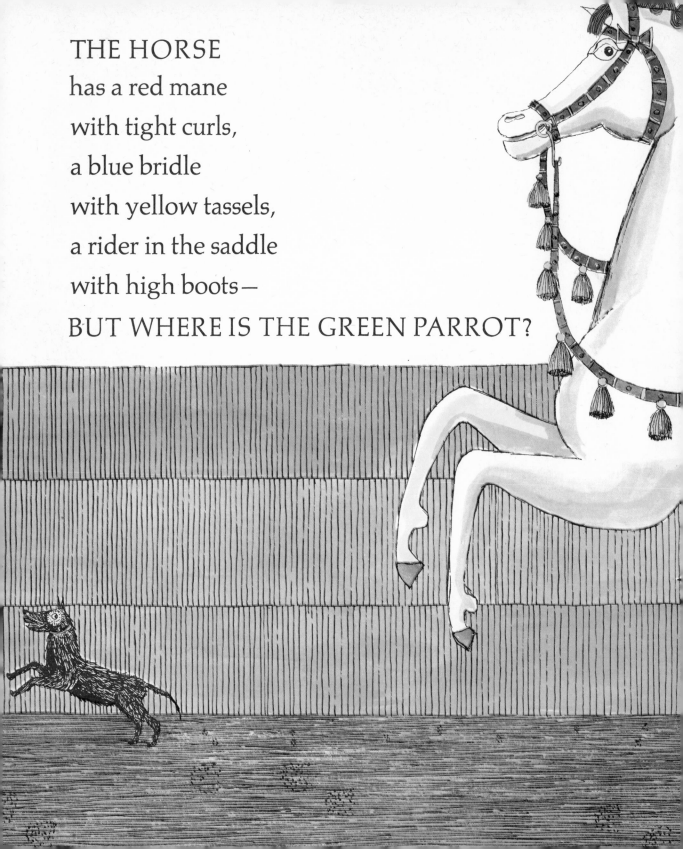

THE SHIP
has a red funnel
with black smoke,
a tall mast
with gay flags,
round portholes—
who is looking out?

AND WHERE
IS THE GREEN PARROT?

THE SKY
has the sun
which sometimes shines,
black clouds
which sometimes rain,
flocks of birds
which always fly—
BUT WHERE IS THE GREEN PARROT FLYING?

Do you know where?

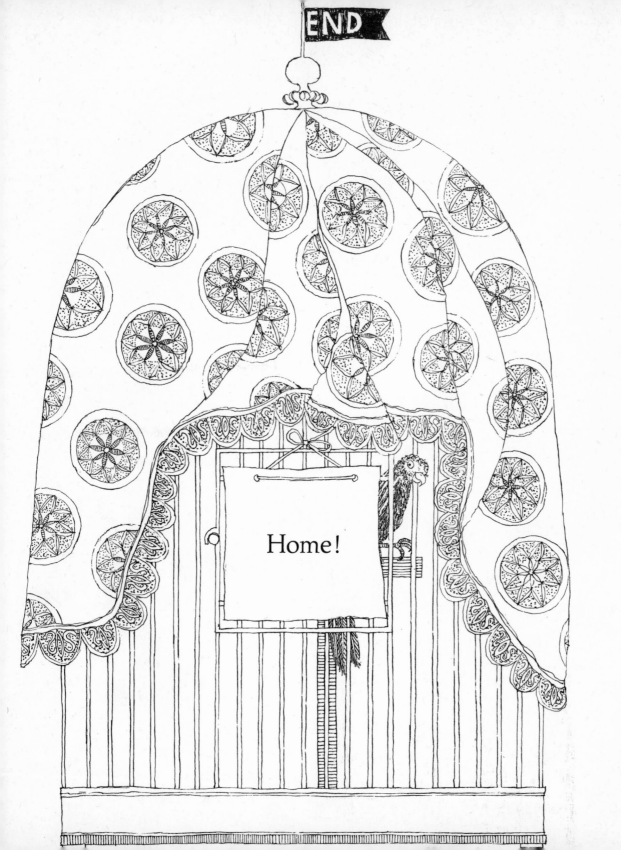